LEAH

Goes Potty

As soon as
breakfast was
over, Leah
ran to play
in her room.

Mom called her back:
“Leah, you need to go potty

Already? Leah did not feel like peeing at all. She was far too busy coloring in her book.

Mom put the potty
next to Leah.

"You do not wear diapers anymore, you're a big girl now," she told her.

Mom helped Leah into a comfortable position.

Leah felt bored sitting on her potty. She got up and looked down at it.

What if she turned the potty into a hat? It would be a lot more fun.

Dad walked into the toilet and laughed when he saw her.

“Leah, that’s not what the potty is for!” he said.

Dad sat Leah on the potty correctly once again. She waited quietly for a while.

Before long, her
hands started
to fidget and her
legs wiggled.

Leah leaped to her feet.

Thump! The potty flipped upside down. Luckily, it was empty!

Leah put it back right side up.

She dashed off to fetch her doll Zoe
and Barnaby, her favorite rabbit.

Oh! Zoe and Barnaby
can sit on the potty.

Leah laid them
down gently.

They will rest while
she goes for a wander.

Ah! But suddenly, Leah needed to pee!

She sped to her potty!

Quick! Zoe and Barnaby,
make room, Leah
is in a hurry.

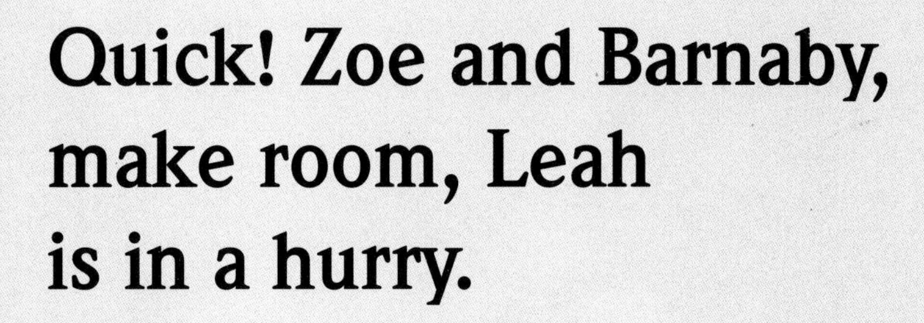

Sigh! Leah got there
just in time.

She showed her parents the potty. Mom and dad clapped excitedly. Good job, Leah!